CONTENTS

Chapter 1: History of the asylums

Chapter 2: In the beginning

Chapter 3: Leaving home

Chapter 4: welcome to your new home

Chapter 5 The laundry

Chapter 6 the Escape

Chapter 7 The lost files

Chapter 8 The hospital

Chapter 9 Eliza May

Chapter 10: The orphanage

Chapter 11: Goodbye Alison

Chapter 12: To my Mother

Chapter 13: To my Sister

Chapter 14: Sports day visit

Chapter 15: Fatal Escape

Chapter 16 Christmas Day

Chapter 17: Humiliation

Chapter 18 Sister Teresa

Chapter 19 : Freedom

CHAPTER 1: History of the asylums

The Magdalene institutions were opened from the 18th century to the late 20th century. They were designed as institutions for fallen women deemed as promiscuous. The majority of women sent there were unmarried mothers who were forced to reside their dew to having a child outside of marriage. Many of the women sent there were seen as unwanted women in society. Often women were sent there by their families and through the churches influence. In this period the church had considerable influence and through the churches powerful status, the church was never criticised and the nuns did what was said. The laundries originated through Europe and North America in the 19th and 20th century with the last laundry closing in 1996. The laundries were named after Mary Magdalene a reformed prostitute. Mary Magdalene had to reject sexuality for her soul to be saved. The girls penance was prayer and remaining in silence, and working long 12 hour day's labour washing and cleaning, purging of sin by washing linen. The institutions were set up in order to chastise and correct the fallen woman who had sold her body for sex, at a time when contraception was illegal and sex education was prohibited, these can be seen as external factors which led to young women becoming pregnant at a young age. Many of the girls following the birth of their child were rejected by their families, there was no welfare support for the young women, and instead the young women were taken into the asylum intuitions as refugees by the nun. The asylums were seen as charitable institutions. In the 1940's the institutions were prominently made up of unmarried mothers. Whilst some women were sent their dew to a suspicion that their chastity had been taken. If a woman's behaviour was seen as promiscuous or even if the young women were seen as being candidates to tempt men they were sent to the asylums. Women in the asylum were stripped of their femininity in being forced to have their hair cut by the nuns, being made to wear wash clothes and had as much rights and freedom as a criminal in prison. The women's baptismal names were changed to holy ones.

The work that the girls undertook was long and laborious, working long hours washing linen, folding sheets with heavy starched linen. Injuries during work were common, some girls were hit if they were not quick enough washing the linen. The nuns in the institutions were seen as god like figures and whatever they commanded or asked, the girls would have to listen to avoid punishment. Loneliness was a common theme in the asylums as friendships were highly discouraged in the asylums. Many of the women were isolated from the outside world. Many of the girls would rebel against the nuns orders committing acts such as smashing windows, punching and kicking out, and they were punished by being physically assaulted by the nuns. There was no way the girls were allowed to leave the asylum. Many remained in the asylums all their lives, and those that finally managed to leave reported that they felt their respectability had gone. The women were allowed no recreation or books or magazines as any form of enjoyment was prohibited. Many women once leaving the asylum described feeling frightened, being felt like they were being watched, carrying a guilt and shame bestowed upon them from the nuns in the asylums. Some of the women were tracked down by sympathetic relatives and were released from the asylums.

As many women became pregnant before marriage the child was seen as being lost and were sent to orphanages next door to the Magdalene asylums for the pardoning of their sins. The young children were warned against talking to the Magdalene girls. The women were branded by society as 'bad' 'devils' and 'sinners' almost as if they were an inferior group. The laundries were run by four religious congregations for over 200 years, 30,000 women lived and worked in the laundries in Ireland. Many women sent to the asylums reported the abuse and injustice that they suffered from the religious orders. The last laundry closed in 1996 putting an end to the harrowing treatment endured by the young women. A formal state apology was given in February 2013 in response to the McAleese report which stated the mistreatment of the women in the asylums over a 70 year period. The Irish police failed to protect the workers, as the women were never paid in the laundries for their service. The Magdalene girls have fought a long time for justice and compensation. In the asylum they received no wages and no quality of life for their hard work. The state gave high laundry contracts to the institutions, but did not comply to working directive laws. Edna Kenny the prime minister at the time apologised for the cruelty endured.

CHAPTER 2: In the Beginning

I am Martha Egan was born in 1935 in Dublin Ireland. In 1951 at the age of sixteen I became pregnant and my life was set to change forever. I lived in a small semi-detached house in the town centre with my father a postman, and my mother a housewife, along with my older brother David a carpenter aged seventeen and sister Alice eleven. I was bought up as a strict catholic, me and my family attended church every Sunday, we would have to pray every day before and after meals, and my parents expected us all to uphold our strict moral catholic values. I was never allowed to go out with friends till late, I was warned against drinking alcohol, and my parents would punish us if we used any obscenities.

When I was sixteen I was a shy and awkward teenager, I had two friends at school and became quite introverted to people I did not know. I went to strict Catholic school St Augustus in Dublin, we had strict teachers who were mostly local nuns. We would be punished for the slightest thing from passing a note to whispering to our peers on the next desk. Punishments included twenty hits with the Cain, smacking our hands with the ruler several times, and spending the entire school day in the isolation room. I was a happy child up to the age of sixteen. I enjoyed going to the cinema with my siblings, going on our family boat in the lock, I was a keen gymnast and had won several awards for my achievements. I was a happy normal teenager but the events following my sixteenth birthday were about to shatter my life forever.

On my sixteenth birthday after much persuasion my parents had agreed for me to hold a party at our local youth centre the cavil bar with my school class. It was a great party with a large group of friends, my favourite food, bright florescent lights, flashing on the small dance floor in the bar. During the party I met Jamie Daniels a boy in my class who whispered to me he wanted to show me something in the bar closet. Unfortunately that night being a young naïve teenager and feeling a tremendous amount of guilt after I had lost my virginity that night with Jamie. I would never interact with him face to face following that night. I remember feeling guilt after the night's events being unable to sleep at night, wondering if all my family knew what had happened. Three months had passed and I woke up each morning becoming sick oblivious to the fact that I was having morning sickness. I realised I was gaining weight and so did my parents and school friends. It was at four months when I became increasing bigger I decided to buy a pregnancy test at the local pharmaceutical shop, my worst suspicions were confirmed I was pregnant at sixteen. I could not tell my family, my father would kill Jamie he could even kill me, I feared my mother would abandon me dew to the shame I would bring upon the family. I knew how my parents would react. I remember one morning arriving to our local doctors shaking nervously hoping to gain advice over having an abortion and avert the crisis I was going through. As the receptionist blurted out "Martha Egan the doctor will see you now" I ran straight out of the doctors surgery in floods of tears. I could not go through it for fear of the doctor telling my parent's. A thousand scenarios crept into my mind I could run away and catch a ferry to England and have the baby, I could have the baby and leave it safely at the local hospital. I was unable to think rationally for a girl of my age and living in a strict catholic background, and being pregnant would mean my life would be over shunned by family and community, bringing a disgrace to our parish and school community, and being classed as 'promiscuous' or 'fallen girl'

Following the eight months of my pregnancy I did everything in my power to conceal my secret. Spending all of the birthday money I had saved for years on baggy jumpers and trousers, constantly wearing an overcoat in winter and summer, now wearing an oversized jumper. I had managed to fool my family and friends for so long during the pregnancy, and I became very reclusive spending a lot of time in my room listening to my wireless radio, crying at night with fear and trepidation knowing that once the baby was born my life would be over.

One morning in the middle of conducting a science experiment with Stacey in our Biology class my waters broke. I had never been so terrified my teacher Mrs Shell quickly ushered me to the nurse's office following the whispering of my friends as they called the ambulance. I could hear the echoes as the crowd of school friends gathered around the nurses offices, "She's pregnant she's going into labour" announced Poopy Lavage the most popular girl in my class. The ambulance came and in full view of my peer group and teachers I was taken to the community hospital to give birth. The labour was very traumatic my school nurse Mrs Gabon was present holding my hand supporting me through it. I had given birth to a baby boy 6 pounds 10 but I could not bring myself to look at him. I was hysterical curled in a ball in my small isolated white room. My mother arrived to the hospital I could see her crying behind the rear glass hysterically she looked broken. My mother explained to me I had shamed her and that there would be serious consequences for what I had done, my father stood by bed side in his long black overall coat scowling at me being unable to look at me. "Dad please look at me say something,"

I cried. Instead my farther face was red and filled with rage I had let him down, his eldest daughter, I was left alone that evening requesting not to see the baby, I was devastated and afraid of the uncertainty of my future.

CHAPTER 3: Leaving home

The weeks that followed were very traumatic it was August 1951 and it was my school summer holidays. Instead of enjoying the warm weather going to the beach with my friends I spent the three weeks post pregnancy curled up in my bedroom listening to my wireless radio. I feel like an outcast a black sheep in my own home. My mother barely came to see me, only to leave meals and snacks outside my bedroom door for me to eat being unable to face my family. I never managed to see my son I was afraid, anxious, and worried about attempting to hold or begin to think of taking care of him. My mother had explained to me that by having the baby at such a young age and out of wedlock I had embarrassed her and the entire community. She advised me she couldn't show her face at our local parish, for the fear of whispering and to be seen as the mother of 'the tearaway teenager'. Most shockingly of all my mother explained to me how my son was to be adopted by the young couple across the way from us, who were unable to have children of their own, and that I was to be sent away to live in alternative accommodation, as living with mum and dad was not seen as viable.

I had mistakenly been forced my mother to admit that Jamie Daniels was the father of the baby, as she had insisted to know who the farther was. This was followed by my mother ringing Jamie's mother who quickly stormed over to our house, explaining to my mother that her son would never get involved with such a promiscuous girl and that I should be locked away to prevent other young men being led astray. This angry confrontation was followed by my mother dragging Mrs Daniels by the arm, and throwing her outside of our house in anger.

I had not asked my mother what she had named my Son I could not face him or my farther. I remember the last time I saw my son. I peered through my bedroom window to see the Bradshaw family take my son away in a wide magnificent pram. I could see my son dressed in a blue baby grower, bright blonde curly hair so small and vulnerable. I did not feel a sense of loss or a feeling that I wanted to keep my son. As I watched as Mrs Bradshaw hold my son in her arms, the young 21 year old women seemed ecstatic she could now finally have her own child. Together Mrs Bradshaw and Mr Bradshaw left down the street wheeling my son away. Finally now my son has been adopted I may be able to regain a sense of normality, and surely my parents will find it in themselves to forgive me for what I had done. I could not have been more wrong the adoption of my son was just the beginning of my torment.

It had now been exactly three weeks since I had given birth and being confined to my room. One morning at the end of August my mother burst my door open storming through brazenly in her dark gown and black hat, opening the curtains carrying my suitcase. My mother immediately opened my wardrobe door and started to pack my clothes into the suitcase. "Where am I going" I insisted. My mother's face was solemn and filled with rage as she began to pack my clothes hurriedly into the large brown case. "Please talk to me your treating me as if I were a ghost" I pestered. My mother turned to glance at me. "If only you were a ghost I would not have to look at you again. Imagine my daughter a good catholic girl falling pregnant at sixteen, embarrassing our name and making me and your father look like unfit parents. I'm not prepared for any more of your antics and I don't know what you're capable of doing next. You're going somewhere where you can be helped and your beyond help here Martha I'm afraid to say", she insisted. "Just tell me where I'm going" I screamed. My mother dragged my suitcase out of the room and down the stairs to the front door. My father was dressed in a suit stood at the porch gazing out of the window unable to face looking at me again. My brother too stood at the porch gazing at me disconcertingly, "Do you have any idea what it's like to be related to you, the whole town is talking about you, you're just a tramp" he said looking at me in disgust. I could feel my eyes begin to flood with tears before I knew it my mother dragged me by the hand out the house and into the Rolls Royce. My father followed and went into the car. It was eerily silent in the car I glanced out of the window to see my neighbours peering through the windows hoping to catch a glimpse of the 'fallen girl.' My brother stood at the porch with my younger sister in his arms looking at me as if I was a criminal my younger sister was oblivious to the fact I was leaving. I grabbed onto my father's shoulder as he began to drive slowly out of our street. "Where am I going Da please tell me" I yelled, my farther ignored me and brushed my hand of his shoulder and insisted, "I cannot even look at you never mind talk to you, we will not look after you anymore you need help" He said, as I looked at him tears filled his eyes. I was devastated I felt like a monster like a criminal I wished I could turn back time to my sixteenth birthday, and I would never have met Jamie and been in this awful mess. I was devastated, lost and had never felt so alone.

CHAPTER 4: Welcome to your new home

Farther pulled up outside the laundry house. It was a grand mansion protected with steel gates. I saw the two nuns begin to exist from the front door coming towards us. I knew instantly I had been taken to a place for unruly girls. I use to talk about this with my classmates girls in Ireland being sent away for their sins or for having children before marriage and never leaving them. "I'm not going in there!" I screamed. As my parents left the car I held onto the handle refusing to get out. My farther opened the door and attempted to drag me by my legs out of the car I began to kick and scream holding onto the car seats desperately trying to fight against my father. As I came out of the car I fell to the ground. As I looked up I could see the two nuns stood there looking at me one was a young nun pretty with short blonde cropped hair and the other was an older nun in her late 40's with grey hair tied in her a bun looking at me as if I was an insect with a concerned expression. "I hope you won't kick up a fuss like that with us here, I can see already you will be a handful. I am Sister Eleanor and this is Sister Mary you will be staying with us now." She said wincing at me patronisingly folding her arms. The nun grasped my hand and lifted me from the floor to my feet. My mother preceded to hand my suitcase to Sister Teresa before she and my father went back in the Rolls Royce and began to drive away. My parents did not even look at me as they began to drive away their faces fixed in disgust. I began to walk towards the car attempting to follow them before Sister Mary clenched my arm, "Don't run after them you've caused them enough heartbreak." She stammered. The nuns quickly ushered me into the doors of the big overpowering creepy mansion.

As I entered the mansion I was greeted to a long corridor with five doors and in the middle was large spiral staircases leading to my dormitory were I would meet the other 'fallen girls.' I felt tired and hungry, as I walked with the nuns through the cold dark corridor, fighting back any attempts at crying trying not to show how desperately weak I felt. As we went up the long spiralled staircase, I arrived at my dormitory were I would meet the other six girls I was to be staying with. As I walked into the room I could see the six girls sitting on their beds wearing dreary brown clothed clothes 'peasant clothes' as I would soon call them. The girls included Helena George a girl with bright long ginger curly hair pale and small. Helena was eighteen years old and sent to the dormitory for her unruly behaviour being caught shoplifting in her local supermarket and breaking into her neighbours house. Helena was loud, rebellious, and had a very fiery temper refusing to form any sort of relationship with the other girls

Louise Dreary was seventeen years old, she was tall six foot with long brown hair very pretty and one of the shyest of the girls in the dormitory. Louise had fallen pregnant at sixteen also and her parents had forced her to have her baby in secret and the adoption was completed privately, without any of the town being aware of what had occurred.

Hannah Graham was twenty one years old, being seen to the dormitory at sixteen for setting fire to her father's house, following discovery of his affair and also for being caught having a sexual relationship with her town vicar which she insistently denied, falling pregnant and being forced into having an abortion by her mother. Hannah was very smart and had aspirations to become a dentist always explaining how she would one day escape the laundry and achieve her dream.

Sara Ellen was sent to the laundry aged sixteen following years of disruptive and violent behaviour towards her family and her disruptive behaviour in school. Sara's family had been unable to cope with her violent behaviour, years later Sara Ellen would be diagnosed with ADHD. However her behaviour was deemed as being self-inflicted. Whilst in the laundry Sara made several attempts to escape, such as attempting to steal the guard's keys and attempting to climb the barbed wire fence. Sara Ellen was often placed in the isolation room in the laundry spending all day in solitary confinement as a punishment. The nun's and girls in the laundry were always wary of her often flying out into fits of rage throwing food around at meal times, hitting out at the Nun's, no form of punishment seemed to control Sara Ellen's behaviour.

Louise Edwards was 22 when she entered the laundry, a shy girl with brown short hair very slim and very introverted. Louise Edwards was sent to the asylum dew to her promiscuous behaviour following her mother's passing. Louise got into a bad gang with the girl who she lived with in Cork, being involved in criminal acts such as stealing, starting public riots, and breaking and entering into resident's houses. Bing sent to the laundry had changed Louise's personality forever, as well as being introverted and isolating herself from the other girls, Louise would often go on hunger strikes and would often be force fed by the nuns in the laundry.

Alison Rhymer the oldest of the girls in the dormitory was thirty four years old. Alison was sent to the dormitory aged seventeen following becoming pregnant to twins, Alison was forced to have the twins in private and her family had discovered that the father of the baby was a married man who was a close friend of the family. Alison had fiercely fought and campaigned with her parents that she wanted to look after the twins, but they had refused to give her the right to be a mother.

The dormitory was cold and dreary the walls were tiled and painted black. The beds were close together there was no privacy and no space for any of us.

That night as the other girls were sleeping I stood in front of the large tainted window in the dormitory gazing out into the beautiful moonlit field. In front I could see the wide steel gates to prevent us from escaping. Beyond that I could see the beautiful field, the scenic mountains looked magnificent in the moonlight shadow. I would often climb the mountains with my parents in happier times it now seemed like I would never regain that happiness I once felt. I was trapped and imprisoned in the cold dark dormitory with four other girls. I was terrified feeling completely alone but unaware that this was only the beginning of my nightmare.

CHAPTER 5: The laundry

My first day in 'the asylum' I was woken by a large bell being rung as Sister Teresa bust through in to our room demanding us all to get ready for our morning breakfast. We all got up slowly out of our beds, at the end of my bed I found the brown ghastly rag dress I was to wear for my remaining time in here, gone was freedom of choice or freedom to make my decisions. As we all dressed we proceeded to line up by the dormitory door. "Silence girls!" Sister Teresa shouted as we whispered to each other. All of a sudden Sara Ellen decided to pull Louise's hair in the line resulting in Sister

Teresa blood vessels nearly burst from her face, "anymore and you'll spend the day in confinement" She grumbled. Sara Ellen quickly shot back at sister Teresa with a vacant expression. As we made our way out of the dormitory we were greeted by other girls who were also in a line making their way to the meal room to eat our breakfast in silence. As we made our way to the breakfast table we were seated in tables in rows of 5 with seats for sixty girls. We were all given bowls of cold porridge. I was disgusted I felt I had to force myself to eat the breakfast, at home I would have warm porridge with jam, now the porridge was crunchy chewable and stale. I was hungry but I had no choice I had to eat this. Following breakfast at 10 am we were sent to the laundry work room a large room. The room was boiling hot, with several wash basins with linen and clothes. We would physically have to bend over the basins to wash the linen scrubbing with our hands till they bled often sweating dew to the incredible heat in the room. We were enforced to work in complete silence if were seen to be talking the nuns would start to scowl at us or provide us with a warning. My back ached the first day I worked in the laundry. I had seemed to get nowhere washing mercilessly the linen with soap and water in the basin. Sister Bridget patronisingly made an example of me believing I was incapable of washing the linen and how she could still see dirt mark in the blanket I had just washed. "Look at Martha, She boasted, can't even wash linen such a basic task but lacks the ability to wash linen are you thick Martha?" She scowled. I could feel her beady brown eyes glaring at me with hatred and pity. I quickly nodded my head to agree with her only for her to shout, "Even she agrees girls she is that thick." I was not aware at the time but being made to feel embarrassed and worthless was to be a regular occurrence in the asylum. After working laborious hours in the wash room we went to the meal room to have our main meal. Cold mash potatoes with cold pieces of steak. All of the meals were cold and I was convinced they were not edible to eat. As we sat eating our meal the nuns were crowded around their own table eating luxury 3 course meal, I could see the steam from the warm roast dinner, the mountain of ice cream was piled at the end of the table it was cruel and unjust. I wondered if they were here to just torture us in any way they could imagine.

That afternoon was filled with more hard labour I truly felt I was being punished and wondered how I could cope being locked in the asylum for as long as the other girls had endured. As I began to scrub the corridor with warm water and disinfectant with my large bucket and oversized flannel. A young girl began to whisper to me a young girl about 15. "Your new here she whispered. Just keep your head down get on the wrong side of Sister Teresa she is the wickedest of all, she once left me in the isolation room for 24 hours with no food or water for talking whilst doing laundry," She murmured. "How did you end up here?" I enquired. "I was accused of being promiscuous and a dangerous girl. My class teacher in his 50's called Mr Alex, would often call me back after to complete extra study. He began to touch me inappropriately. Then one afternoon he pushed me in the classroom cupboard attempted to kiss me. I screamed out and the head teacher rushed in. My teacher said I was hysterical disruptive and acting sexually inappropriate to him. Despite my desperate attempts to tell the truth I was accused of lying and was deemed dangerous. My parents believed the school team and I was sent here." "You shouldn't be here you did nothing wrong!" I stammered. "Who is talking down there" fired an angry shrill voice. "My names Martha what is your name? I enquired. "I'm Rebecca and don't worry I'll get us out of here stick with me." She concluded giving me a friendly reassuring smile.

CHAPTER 6: The escape

It was a cold winter's morning November 2nd 1953 I awoke to Rebecca the girl I had met on my first day tugging at my feet. She stood at the end of the bed dressed in her buttoned beige winter coat carrying her suitcase. "What are you doing" I whispered frustrated at being woken up so early. "I promised you we would get out and today is the day!" she beamed. "Are you crazy? It will never work we will get caught" Rebecca came to sit in my bed, "no we won't I stole the guards keys last night, it has the keys for all the doors in the laundry if you don't come with us now you can stay in here and rot till you're an old women" she pleaded. I gazed at her I admired her determination and in the spur of the moment I thought this is it, if I don't attempt to escape here now I may never leave here I was willing to take the risk. I quietly stumbled out of bed, changed from my night clothes into the rags, and with Rebecca made my way to the dormitory door. When all of sudden Sara Ellen tiptoed behind us, "what are you doing your escaping" she whispered. Rebecca's smile turned to rage as she turned to face her "Yes we are if you make one sound or rat us out I swear I will make you pay for it" she scowled. "If you don't let me escape with you I'll scream the place down and none of us will be leaving" She persisted. "Ok hurry up and get your day clothes on we only have one hour before wakeup call don't make a sound," Said Rebecca reluctantly. I stood there by the door with Rebecca both looking at each other disapprovingly, if it wasn't enough that both of us were attempting to escape, Sara Ellen was a loose cannon and was a big risk in us getting caught, but she found out we had no choice but to include her in the escape plan . Sara finished packing her satchel and moved slowly towards us. Rebecca turned to us, "Right listen we need to move very slowly down the spiral stairs As soon as we reach the bottom we need to run for the front door ill open it then once the door is closed we run to the main gates which I will open, whilst one of you guards the door. As soon as we get out we have to climb the fence, but you both need to be fast or we won't make it!" "Let's do it" I whispered determined that Rebecca's well thought out plan would work. We slowly made our way out of the dormitory, we huddled together as we slowly made our way down the long spiral staircase. I could feel my heart beating rapidly, the sweat was pouring own my face. I was aware that if I was caught sister Teresa and the other nuns would make me pay for it and I'd never be allowed to leave the asylum. I could be permanently isolated in the quiet room. All three of us slowly made it down the spiral staircase. As soon as we reached the bottom we ran with Rebecca leading. I felt my heart was going to beat out of my chest, I was terrified, filled with adrenaline and excitement at the same time. Rebecca opened the door and we made our way out. I guided the front door for sounds of the guards, whilst Rebecca and Sara opened the security gate.

Once opened we ran for the bristled nettle bush and fence we had to cross to our freedom. This was it I've got to get out of here I have no plan ahead but it's the first step. Rebecca turned to Sara who started to climb the bristled nettle fence her hands bleeding from the nettles. "Are you crazy cutting yourself on there is there any other way out?" Questioned Sara Ellen. "Just cross it, do it now or you'll never leave c'mon" pleaded Rebecca. Rebecca with steely determination managed to cross the fence to the open field encouraged us to come along. Sara began to cross the fence gasping as the nettles pulsated into her skin. I started to cross the fence I felt the nettles inject into my bare arms and legs as they started to bleed. All of sudden I heard a loud voice beam out from behind me, "Stop them girls don't let them leave!" It was Sister Teresa she was frantic with rage. As the guards charged towards us. Sara reached the top of the fence and jumped into the field crying out in pain. "C'mon Martha!" cried Rebecca as the guards began to reach out to grab me. My hands reached the top of the fence when all of a sudden I felt one of the guards grab my feet. Instantly pulling me down the nettles further pulsated through my skin causing my face now to be cut and bleed. The guard held me on the floor. I could see Rebecca and Sara running in the field running to their freedom. Sister Teresa stood and shouted in frustration, "The guards are coming for you girls there is no escape nowhere to hide you will suffer for this." Sister Teresa turned to me her long white straggly hair sweeping across her face, she scowled at me and charged towards me as the guard held me down by the cusp of my collar. I was shaking I was crying in pain, I was devastated to have been caught, and felt now I was going to suffer more than I had done before. Sister Teresa began to slap me hard across the face with her black shoes. "Stop I shouted, you evil sadistic cow" I blurted out in rage. "It's funny the other two managed to get away but the thickets girl couldn't even climb a fence well you will be punished now" she gritted through her teeth smiling menacingly at me. The guard brought me to my feet and he dug his large fat hands into my arm and dragged me back into the asylum. For the first time since being in the asylum I began to cry I felt defeated, I was close to freedom, but had I not have guarded the door, if I just climbed over the fence faster I could have escaped.

CHAPTER 7: The Lost Files

As I spent the afternoon locked in Sister Teresa's office and being strictly told not to touch any items in her office. I became more inquisitive I wondered what she had to hide. I decided to search the office discreetly. As I opened one of the filing cabinets I came across a file in a red folder titled, 'Teresa's file' in the file contained names and descriptions of girls who had attended the asylum and their destinations following their departure. The first file was of a girl named Louise Hamilton aged 17, who was taken to the asylum following a miscarriage. Despite losing the child Louise was sent to the asylum. On the record was a behaviour chart describing Louise as a depressed girl with multiple cuts across her arms following several suicide attempts. In the report written by the nun at the time Sister Imelda, it states that Louise suffered night disturbances and would have dreams about the baby she lost. On psychiatric evaluation it was found that Louise was suffering from post natal depression. At the end of the chart it stated Louise was taken out of the asylum by her uncle five years later.

The second file I retrieved was a girl named Abigail smith sent to the home in 1940 following multiple robbery and assault in her hometown of Cork aged 16. In the file it stated how Abigail had committed robbery by breaking and entering into various homes in cork stealing thousands of pounds worth of jewellery, money and antiques. Once When Abigail was caught from an attempt at robbing a home in her neighbourhood she was caught by a policeman Mr Roberts. In the report it states that Abigail spat at the policeman and physically punched him in the face causing a laceration to his left eye. Abigail had previously escaped the orphanage she was residing in Cork aged 14 and had been sleeping rough in her area for two years following her capture. Under agreement by the owner of the orphanage Abigail was sent to the asylum. In the report by the nun sister Dominoes it describes Abigail's behaviour as uncontrollable, with reports of her hitting out at other girls in the asylum, hitting scratching and punching. At the end of the file it stated Abigail had attempted to escape two years after being sent to the asylum, and threw herself in front of a high speed bus the first day she had escaped, she was killed instantly. Abigail had no one to turn to; no family or friends to support her, and suicide felt like the best option states the report.

As I looked through other reports in the file I was startled and in shock when I discovered one report it was Sister Brenda, she had been a Magdalene girl she herself was sent to the asylum! I read in shock the shocking details about Brenda's entry into the asylum. Brenda was sent to the asylum after falling pregnant at the age of 17, in the report it states that Brenda had accused her parish priest farther Henley of raping her, but no evidence was found and Brenda was found to be lying by her family, and sent to the asylum, whilst the baby was sent to an orphanage upon birth. The report of Brenda's behaviour states that she had been an asset to the nuns in the asylum, offering to help the nuns even preparing meals for them, even being described as a mentor to other girls in the asylum, reporting to the nuns about the girl's behaviour, and attending meetings in the asylum with the nuns. At the end of the report it stated that Teresa had been granted permission to reside in the asylum and train as a nun. After one year she had trained and became sister Teresa, in the report it stated that Sister Teresa was an exceptional figure who was role model to the other Magdalene girls, in being seen as an example of being able to reform her life following committing a sin .I felt sickened and angry following reading Sister Teresa's report knowing that she had been through what I had been through, abandoned by her family, made an outcast, and still she inflicts pain and physical suffering on me and the other girls in the asylum, she was a hypocrite, she truly was a monster. As I reread Teresa's file in shock I heard a key turn someone was about to enter the office. I quickly placed the file in the cabinet and rushed over to sit in the chair by the nun's desk. Sister Teresa entered as I nervously sat there. Sister Teresa walked around the office and gazed at the cabinet, I had realized I forgot to close the cabinet door where I had placed the file in. I felt sickened I knew she would now know I knew her secret, what will she do? There's no way she'll let me get away with this. "I see you have found yourself some reading material to occupy since I left you here and you remember me warning you not touch my documents?" Said Sister Teresa mischievously. "I'm so sorry sister!" I blurted. I was shaking all over including my hands and legs I was terrified. I watched as Sister Teresa took the belt from her trousers. She moved closer to me and began to hit me viscously with the belt across my face and body. I stood up and attempted to run for the door when she grabbed me with both hands taking me to the ground. She slapped me hard against my face and with both hands began to squeeze my neck. I could feel myself begin to lose my breath. Sister Teresa's face was boiling read with anger, "You listen to me Martha if you tell anyone about what you've read in those files, your life will not be worth living, I will keep you in isolation permanently for the rest of your time here you understand"! She roared. "Yes" I gasped. Sister Teresa released me from her grasp I realised now that I had made a grave mistake, sister Teresa was going to make me suffer reading the files whether I told the other girls or not.

CHAPTER 8 The hospital

Ever since I resided in the asylum I witnessed many of the girls gain several injuries from their time in working within the laundries. I watched a girl trip on the slippery floor, scald themselves with hot water and even observed one girl get her hand caught in a spinning wheel. The injury I received however was inflicted by another girl in the laundry, Rebecca Sampson. Rebecca Sampson was a strong big built girl aged 18 she was 13 stone 6 foot tall, with a large round pale face with long messy blond curly hair. Rebecca had been sent to the laundry following a violent attack where she had threated her head teacher with a kitchen knife following a meeting with her about her bullying. It was then decided by her parents, the teacher, and her parish priest that attending the asylum would be the best form of punishment for her uncontrollable behaviour. I was standing over the large heavy basin after five long hours of working in the laundry when all of sudden Rebecca came behind me and proceeded to twist my arm. "You've taken it" She screamed. "I haven't taken anything let go of me!" I pleaded gasping. "You have you stole my best hair brush I found it in your draw, no one steal my things and gets away with it" She shouted. I was terrified and shocked at her behaviour especially as this was all over a brush. I was confused as to why she was becoming angrier. All of a sudden she began to turn on the boiling hot water and went on to fill up the basin. Then Rebecca grabbed my bare arms and forced them into the hot water. I screamed I was in unbearable pain I could see my bare arms changed from white to red as the hot water began to tear at my skin and scald me. Sweat was pouring from my face and I felt dizzy weak and began to scream out in agony. Sister Mary Rushed over, "Rebecca stop this immediately STOP!" She shouted. Then Rebecca began to loosen her tight fatty fingers from my arm and I collapsed suddenly onto the ground. I lay there in pain as I gazed up, I could see the other girls crowd around me and I passed out.

I awoke in a private room in a hospital ward in a bare empty room with white walls and with a huge window in front of me. Through the window I could observe the nurses and doctors rushing past me. I was sat in the room with a guard from the asylum Mark, he was a short chubby man with a large moustache and a stern demeanour. I looked up at my arms they were heavily bandaged in white casting I could barely move them and I was still in unbearable pain. "When will I be allowed to leave here?" I asked the guard. He did not respond. "Have my family been to seen me at all?" I asked. Marks expression turned to anger, "I do not know when you will be coming out I am here to make sure you come back I have been given special instructions to watch you by Sister Teresa" he said robotically. I stopped all means of communication with the security guard that afternoon knowing that he would not help me in any way. The day dragged for me in the hospital that afternoon until my hospital room door opened and my grandma and my sister appeared. I was ecstatic to see my Grandma and sister I immediately blurted out "you've come to take me home!"

My grandma looked elegant wearing a long black evening dress, her blonde hair tied up into a neat bun. My sister stood beside her walking sheepishly to the chair beside my bed. "No we have not come to take you home. We have come to see how you are, now your farther does not know we are hear but I can't stand to see you in pain. Your father does not feel its right for you to leave the asylum yet" Said Grandma. I began to cry uncontrollably, "Grandma please take me home I cannot stand another day in the asylum I am treated like an animal, a slave, I do not deserve to be persecuted," I pleaded. My grandma began to tell me how my brother was now in London studying medicine, whilst also telling me my mother was pregnant but has decided to give up the child for adoption. I was shocked at how much had changed since I'd been gone and how so little had changed for me I was still a prisoner. I tried to evoke my little sister to talk to me but she sat there avoiding all eye contact with me, I felt she had been brainwashed against me I had looked after her as a baby, fed her, watched her take her first steps now she was afraid to talk to me. As my grandma left that afternoon I felt considerable pain and loneliness. I shouted for her to get me out of the asylum but she ignored me and exited the hospital room. That was the very last time I would see my grandmother and little sister again. I spent two weeks in the hospital and upon my discharge I still had the bandages attached having had third degree burns following the attack. I saw Rebecca in the asylum on my return. I could see she had been punished her head was completely shaven, but her behaviour continued to worsen following my attack. Rebecca had bullied and attacked several other girls in the dormitory and was sent to a psychiatric unit and I never saw her again. Even though my arms were severely burnt and I was in considerably burnt I was still expected to undertake laundry duties. Seeing my grandma and sister, and seeing their hostility and refusal to help me made me feel more isolated and afraid.

Chapter 9: Eliza May

After the girls escaped it was not long before their places were filled. Eliza May entered the asylum shortly after the escape. Eliza may was 15 years old she was sent to the asylum dew to a major incident that occurred in her home in Cork. Eliza had become increasingly rebellious following the passing of her mother and when her farther decided to remarry her aunt. Eliza started to skip school, and was caught stealing in the supermarket, Eliza became very aggressive towards the teachers in her schools, lashing out and spitting refusing to remain quiet in lessons Eliza became rude and disobedient. Eliza's behaviour accumulated to one fatal night which would change her future forever. Eliza's farther had expressed to her on a Sunday afternoon that he was to marry Eliza's Aunt Mary, unexpectedly following six months of being in a secret relationship. Eliza reacted very aggressively to this news and at 2am the same night Eliza poured petrol around the kitchen surfaces setting fire to the house. As Eliza ran outside to avoid the flames, her father managed to carry out a severely burnt Mary out of the burning house. Mary had suffered third degree burns to her right arm being caught in the fire. Following this event Eliza's father attempted to keep Eliza's actions secret dew to fear of tarnishing the families' name. Eliza's family priest had advised her farther to send her to the Magdalene asylum in order to correct her behaviour.

Eliza however had come into the asylum kicking and screaming attempting to bite and kick the guards. I could tell Eliza was not going to last in the asylum that she would break under the pressure. Eliza's appearance was very unkempt her short brown her was dirty and crazy, Elisa had scratches all over her arms and legs and appeared dirty in appearance. We would all suffer at night with Eliza in the asylum, if we were trying to sleep Eliza would began to sing out loud, or jump on another girls bed to gain attention. During the day in the laundry Eliza would often stand in the corner with her arms folded defiant she was not going to participate in the laundry service. Often Eliza would clean for one hour spending the majority of the day in isolation. I remember her defiantly throwing a cold bucket of water over one of the nuns in revenge for their behaviour towards her. However no form of punishment be it being locked in the isolation room, being physically hit by the nuns or being starved could deter Eliza's behaviour. Eliza would often disrupt prayer practice by singing songs in order to aggravate the nuns and create tension. Eliza would not follow any rules and made life very difficult for the girls and nuns in the asylum as being punished would make her more rebellious and more physically hostile. I remember sitting with Eliza a week before she left us asking why she continued to rebel and suffer being hit by the nuns being locked up in the isolation rooms and disrupting the atmosphere in the asylum. Eliza explained, "I have nothing to live for my mother died in a car accident with my old sister last year and life is not worth living, my farther has forgotten they existed, I just want to be with them my life truly finished when they died." She sniffled crying into my shoulder. As aggressive and erratic as Eliza was I could also tell from our outburst that she was very vulnerable and was in need of psychiatric help. The nuns and guard staff had branded Eliza as crazy and beyond help. Eliza's last day culminated in a battle between herself and Sister Teresa. We all had finished a long day in the laundry and sat down for supper. I had been surprised that afternoon that Eliza had become very complaint with completing washing duties scrubbing the floor and participating in all activities without hesitation. I was very suspicious of Eliza's sudden change in behaviour. As we all began to pray before our meals Eliza had a rope behind her back. I watched as she walked up slowly to the nun's dining table. "Sit down Eliza" Mary shouted. "Eliza you're impressing no body with your behaviour sneered Sister Teresa. All of a sudden Eliza appeared behind Sister Teresa placing the rope behind her neck and attempted to strangle her. Teresa was pulling at the rope the other nuns attempted to prize Eliza's fingers grip from the rope, however Eliza began to bite out at the nuns, until eventually the guards managed to pull an angry and determined Eliza away from Sister Teresa. Sister Teresa collapsed breathlessly on the floor. "You'll pay for this Eliza you'll be sent now away to the mental hospital we will see how smart you are then" Shouted a boiling angry sister Mary. Eliza was dragged by the guards from the dining room to the dormitory in a fit of rage. The guards stayed with her until the staff from the mental hospital arrived to take Eliza away. When the medical staff from the mental institution arrived to take Eliza away she put up an enormous fight to try to escape. Eliza held onto the bedposts with almighty force. The four men were able to carry Eliza crying hysterically out of the dormitory room and to the medical hospital, where she was placed in a psychiatric unit. Sister Teresa paid a visit to our dormitory that night, advising the girls that if we were ever to behave in such an aggressive way as Eliza we would be sent away. I felt worried and almost missed Eliza when she left. Although she was suffering following the death of her family members, Eliza fought right to the very end in her time at the asylum. I had heard years later that Eliza had died in the mental hospital following years of self-neglect and refusing to eat. A part of me had wished Eliza had got rid of Sister Teresa once and for all, however I could not contain such angry feelings I had to remain strong.

Chapter 10 The orphanage

The children's orphanage next to the asylum had ben of great interest to all of the girls in the asylum. Especially as many of the girls had expressed that there children had been seen to the asylum and that they had even expressed that they had witnessed seeing them from the windows of the dormitory. This was true of Angela in my dormitory who expressed to me that she had seen her twins in the asylum, and knew they were hers having seen the resemblance and vowing to one day getting her son and daughter out of the asylum. When I was in the gardens sometimes I could hear the nuns warn the children not too look over the fence to the girls in the asylum. I would overhear the nuns describe us as devils, as evil characters, and the children were warned if they spoke to us they would become sinners. It was forbidden for the girls in the asylum to talk to the children in the orphanage and if anyone was seen to make contact they were warned they would be severely punished. One afternoon I remember scrubbing the floors in the dormitory when I heard one girl shout, "Martha look Angela's trying to escape over the fence why is she going to the orphanage?" said Sara in bewilderment. I got up and could see as Angela had climbed up the fence reaching the top with almighty force. Two hours later Angela had returned to the dormitory and had spoken to me about what she witnessed. "I saw my children!" she gasped. "You did?" I quizzed. "It was definitely them Stacey and Michael they were beautiful. They were so alike of course I couldn't tell them who I was but at least I got to see them, I know I will meet them again one day but it feels great to have met my grown children." She beamed. I watched her he desperation on her face the loss she had felt since losing her children and how happy she was meeting them. For many of the children in the asylum entering our asylum was a progression once they entered adulthood. The children were seen as being sinners from being born by the unmarried mothers. The girls that entered the asylum from the orphanage reported working longer hours being abused and assaulted by the nuns, it had seemed no different to the asylums except the children had spent their entire life in the asylum. A girl who entered the asylum was Rebecca Fitzgerald she was treated very differently from the other girls in the orphanages. Rebecca did not share a dormitory with the other girls and was often observed going into a private room. Sister Teresa's behaviour towards Rebecca was very peculiar I would often observe Rebecca going into the office with Teresa for others, at other times I would observe Teresa embracing Rebecca even praising her for hard work in the dormitory. It was later on that I would discover that Rebecca was Teresa's secret daughter she had had aged 16 no one ever knew no one ever guessed.

Chapter 11: Goodbye Alison

Alison Rhymer was one of the older girls in the laundry figure, she became a mother figure to the girls in the dormitory, whenever we were upset, really missing home, or needed someone to help us keep carm Alison would always help us. Alison was a true example of the effects staying in the laundry would have upon us. Alison had been in the asylum for over fifteen years and the hard work and heavy labour had aged her before her time. Alison's hair was bright grey, her face was wrinkled and grey in colour. Alison had deep varicose veins in her legs, she would often walk around bent over as she suffered from chronic back pain, from bending over the basin for years and scrubbing the floors. At night if ever I was awake, I would see Alison at times withering in pain in her bed her face contorted in pain. Despite the torture and abuse Alison had endured from the nuns, she had never once rebelled against them, she always remained polite courteous and respectful even though we had never been treated with respect. Alison had seemed to me like one of the strongest willed girls I had ever met, resilient to being locked away, that all changed after one night in the dormitory. I remember the night very clearly, it was the beginning of October it was much colder than usual and the boiler had broken in the asylum, so it was particularly cold this night. I could see a light on in the girl's bathroom and I could hear a shrill cry. I stumbled out of bed tiptoed across the hard floorboards and walking into the bathroom, I was started to see Alison with a rope around her neck standing on the edge of the bath ready to take her own life. I jumped up onto the bath edge and held the rope attached to Alison. "I need to get you out of this Alison we can't lose you your stronger than this" I cried. Alison started to cry hysterically as I began to unravel the rope around her neck. All of sudden on the bathroom wall two dark shadows towered over us. "What's going on here girls" beamed the voice; it was Sister Mary and Teresa. Alison stumbled to her feet and collapsed into a heap. "Trying to take your own life Alison is a mortal sin and Alison and you've already committed a big sin before, you will need to come to the isolation room for you own safety" shouted Sister Teresa. Sister Mary nodded in agreement. "I'm not going in there you'll have to drag me there!" cried Alison hysterically. I had never seen Alison appear like this before after years of being locked in the dormitory it appeared to me that she was having a mental breakdown. Ten minutes later Alison was dragged by Sister Mary and two other nuns out of the dormitory and into the isolation room. All the girls in the dormitory watched in horror as Alison was taken down to isolation, if Alison was not going to cope how could any of us?

Usually girls were sent to the isolation for one day, and usually after this they would return carmer, after having time to think about their behaviour and complete their penance. However Alison had resided in the isolation room for seven whole days. Alison's transformation mentally and physically after being isolated shocked all the other girls. Once a figure for support Alison became a shell of her former self, she became reclusive, self-isolated and extremely depressed. During work she would greet us only saying 'hello' her bright smile had turned into a constant cold frown. Alison appeared vacant almost like a robot. As months passed on during isolation, her chronic back pain had worsened and she would walk around with a wooden walking stick. Her long grey hair had disintegrated as chunks of her hair had fallen out Alison had developed Alopecia. Then one week Alison s pain had worsened so much she was confined to bed rest with the doctors coming to give her treatment daily. I remember Alison looking up to the doctor asking "Am I dieing?" to no response from the doctor. I tried to engage with Alison when she became confined to her bed but she instead turned her back towards me as she turned in the bed. Alison had almost given up on human kind, and without Alison's support I felt more isolated than ever.

One afternoon whilst scrubbing the floors in the nuns office I heard a loud ringing noise it was the fire alarm in the asylum. The nuns had blown their whistles which meant all the girls in the dormitory would have to line up in four vertical lines by the fire exit. The fire alarm going off had always been a secret treat to the girls, a half hours break whilst the guard men would investigate the asylum for anything suspicious. As we all began to walk outside of the asylum waiting for further instructions a large voice boomed from the rooftop. It was Alison dressed in a white night dress and bare footed she began to pray out loud as she stood right at the edge of the roof. "Our farther who art in heaven," The nuns looked up all dithering in panic, "Alison don't move an inch don't go any further. Quick two of you go up there and get her down for Christ's sake!" blurted Sister Teresa. As Sister Sara and Sister Teresa arrived at the rooftop Alison stopped praying, lifted her arms and proceeded to jump from the rooftop. I remember the loud thud as she landed in a heap by the entrance in the asylum. Some of the girls collapsed in horror watching her lifeless body laying on the floor. I began to shake, I was in complete shock. The nuns placed a large blanket over Alison's body. It was very difficult losing Alison there was no memorial following her death, we were advised by Sister Teresa not to talk about the event that occurred that day. Alison was a great help to me in the asylum I felt so lost now that she was gone. I t made me wonder if I would suffer the same fate one day, just how much longer can I be stuck in this awful asylum I wondered.

CHAPTER 12: Dear Mother

Thursday 8th October 1952

Dear Mother,

Today marks my 17th birthday which means I have now spent one year in the Magdalene laundry. I really miss you and farther and my brother and sister. Mother I do not know how much longer I can take it here. My hands are bruised and cut from cleaning and scrubbing the floors I am working twelve our days up at 5am in the morning and finishing work at 7pm the same day. I am suffering from chronic back pain and I really need medical assistance in a hospital where I can be treated properly for this. I feel constantly tired, tearful and isolated. I have so many dreams mother of things I want to do in life, going to college becoming a lawyer and one day getting married. Mother please do not deny me the opportunity to have a normal life. I am surviving on a basic diet of cold soup and bread and mash potatoes. I miss your home cooking the Sunday roasts. I miss my friends at home going to the park walking Ollie, we are lucky to have even a half hour of fresh air each day here. I have always been an outside person, and I miss our farm going out for long walks with father, here I am not gaining any exercise the long hours mean all of my energy is being used up, I am begging you to give me a chance and to get me out of the laundry. I am truly sorry for the sin I have committed, I could never bring myself to accept I am a mother and I am truly ashamed I have inflicted so much pain and misery on you and farther. If I could turn back time and erase what had happened I would I have made a truly terrible poor decision, and I truly feel I have paid my penance being here for the past year. I want to be free from here free from being hit by the nuns, working like a slave till I fear I am going to collapse. I will complete all the housework at home give all my earnings when I get a job to you and father, just please let me come home. If you allow

me to come home at least then I can complete my exams, get a job at Yvette's dry cleaners, and live with Yvette and pay rent. I just want to come home finish my education before it's too late. I have no life here mother I am just existing. I realised I missed your 50th birthday what did you do? I know we had always planned to go to Lourdes on your birthday and I was wondering if you had decided to go. If you have not managed to go I would really like us to go on my 18th birthday. As soon as I leave here I can make a fresh start for myself and make you proud.

Yours sincerely,

        Martha.

CHAPTER 13: To My Sister

Letter from my brother

For five years I had never received a response from my letter. I had hoped a few weeks after reading my letter my mother would come running to the asylum realizing her and father made a mistake sending me here, two years later I received a letter from my brother on my 21st birthday.

Dear Martha,

I know it has been five years since I have seen you. I am now in my final year of medicine school at king college London and hoping to work in Belfast hospital when I come home next year. I really hope you are doing well, and there is not a day that goes by when I don't think about you. Your letter arrived at our house but Ma never opened it, da had thrown it out but luckily I managed to get it. I want you to know I do not feel any anger towards you or blame you for what happened, I hope one day when I finish my studies I will be granted permission to come and get you out there, so you can start a life for yourself. Since you went away things became very difficult at home, Da lost his job in the cold mining factory, Ma had to do extra shifts at Bettie's café as well as taking sis to school. Da was unemployed for two years and spent a lot of time drinking getting himself into a state in 'murphy's bar' each night. Da became ill will psoriasis in hospital last year, but now things are looking up for him now he's gained employment as a scafholder. It's lovely here in London Martha, sightseeing with friends, travelling on my bike exploring the city, going to various music festivals in the city. I could really see myself staying here maybe in a few years we can all move here making a better life for ourselves. Martha please stay strong where you are and know that you have support outside and I will see you again one day. I promise when I finish my studies I will push to get you out I promise.

Best wishes,

    Ben

I had felt more lost than I had been before receiving a letter from my brother. I was upset that my parents would rather throw my letter away than give me a chance. I was also angry in a way that my brother was in London pursuing his dream, whilst I am still here in the asylum 5 years later still being treated like an animal and persecuted for being an unmarried mother. Why should my life be on hold till my brother finishes his studies? Am I now completely dead to my parents? Invisible? How much more can I take. I lay in my bed that night sobbing, instead of providing me with comfort the letter had left me feeling more alone and isolated than before. I also reminded myself that I need to stay positive if I sink into depression I may suffer the same fate as Angela.

CHAPTER 14 : Sports Day

Visit

Sports day was held each year at the asylum on July the 2nd. It was to me a tedious affair watching the nuns put on sports games such as the egg and spoon race, cross country race in the ten acre field, hoopla hoop contests, finding the hidden gold coins. Apparently the sports day was a charity event held by the nuns to raise funds for the asylum to support the girl's educational needs. I could never see how any amount of money the nuns could raise would support our quality of life. Our education was delivered by nuns who delivered educational topics through fear and intimidation and distorted certain topics to benefit their own beliefs.

This sports day at the age of 21 was to become a day I would never forget with an unexpected visitor arrived at the gates at the asylum. It was 10am, the sun shone over the beautiful 10 acre playing field in the asylum gardens. Members of the public had come to observe the sports day activities and sat down on the wooden chairs to watch and observe the fallen girls. It felt at the time to me that members of the public were laughing at us, ridiculing us ,we believed the public had shared the same opinion of us as the nuns in the asylum. As I completed the egg and spoon race with the other girls I had begun to feel silly, I was six foot tall wearing these dirty rags, completing a childish activity in front of the sneers and ridiculing of the nuns and the public. Even on a happy occasion such as the sports day the nuns could still make us feel worthless. At the end of the race standing behind the back gate in the garden was a familiar figure ushering me to come over. It was Sara Bradshaw the lady across the way in my street that adopted my son. I was shocked to see her that day she was wearing a long black duffle coat with white hooped earrings and hair tied up neatly in a bun. Most shocking of all was beside Sara was a small child. I quickly realised this must be my son. At first when I heard her call my name instantly recognising who she was I felt like running away, I did not intend to see her, and certainly not my own child who had led to the persecution and suffering I had endured. For once sister Mary and Sister Teresa seemed so enthralled in sports day I realised that maybe if I went to speak to her for a few minutes they would not notice. I slowly walked up to the gate and there he was my son. As I looked at him I could instantly see a resemblance of his father's Jamie. He had short blond spiked hair, very pale skin dressed in his school uniform. At first he appeared shy digging his hands into Sara. I was in shock and could feel myself trembling, knowing that he was my child, a growing child now at school. "What are you doing here" I snapped awkwardly, finding it hard to know how to communicate with Sara the adoptive mother of my child,or even to recollect why she had come to see me. "I had to visit you I was speaking to Rebecca a few years back and she spoke to me about all the physical abuse you are all suffering here, and I feel appalled, that you've been sent here all because of what happened. I just had to see you to offer my support and felt you had a right to see Jamie." She began to wrap her arms around my son. "There is nothing good going to come out of you visiting me if you can't get me out. I have a terrible life I'm starving most of the time, I'm shivering myself to sleep most of the night, I am working 12 hour shifts cleaning 7 days a week. I'm tired and exhausted, and you come here to offer your support as a free person who can do what they want in their life, I do not want to be patronised." I shouted. I began to storm off stomping my feet out of anger and frustration. "Please don't go" Sara pleaded smiling at me. I also wanted you to know your Ma is not mad at you. She came to visit me and Jamie and she said the only reason she has not contacted you was because of your father, she wants you to know she forgives you but is not permitted to see me" She advised. "Why see me at all then why can't my mother forgive me myself, you're not helping me your making things worse!" I yelled.

"Please try and understand I only came here, to tell you that if you need money or support or a place to stay when you leave you have me. I want you to have this you can hide it under your pillow your mother wanted you to have it." She insisted. Sara had handed me a photo of me on the beach in bundoren when I was 12. In the picture I am burying da in the sand, whilst my brother and sister are building a sandcastle with my ma beside us. It was one of my favourite holidays and a memory I will take with me for the rest of my life. As I turned over the picture I read the message my mother had left me. 'To Martha happy birthday. I 'FORGIVE YOU' love ma.' I began to cry just receiving a message from my mother had made me feel happy knowing they she was not angry with me. "Thank you"! I gasped wiping the tears from my face. Sara smiled and then holding my sons hand she walked off disappearing down the country lane path. All of a sudden a hand snatched the photo out of my hand it was Sister Mary. She gazed at the photo angrily with disgust. "Sister Teresa come here, where did you get this girl. Communicating with people outside the asylum is not permitted!" She scorned. Sister Teresa walked towards us looking at the picture she shook her head at me. She gazed at me angrily her horse shaped teeth gritting in defiance. "How much longer are you going to keep breaking the rules here Martha, first you try to run away, your late for meals and now you think it's acceptable to be keeping silly pictures of you on a beach. Well you won't see it again and you'll be coming to my office at 7am tomorrow for your punishment" Teresa began to tear up the photo in front of me into tiny pieces I watched as the wind blew the pieces away. I was punished the next day Sister Mary held me down whilst Teresa shaved my head completely. I was bald I felt I had lost all of my femininity. The other nuns and girls laughed and jeered at my new appearance. It was at that time I felt so completely low I felt like contemplating suicide, if there was going to be no way out for me surely it would be better not to exist at all?

CHAPTER 15: Fatal Escape

I was 23 years old. Spending seven years inside the asylum had felt like a lifetime. I had begun to struggle to remember my life previously from being ion the asylum. I had spent years longing to be home with my family my feeling of loneliness had now changed to feeling numb with emotion. I had accepted to myself that my family were never going to get me out, my brother would now have had finished medical school, and he is still not here to set me free. I had lost all hope and almost given up on myself. One day on a cold Novembers morning, I was in the garden I saw the back gate was open, the guards must have forgotten to lock the door. I was perplexed as to why the gate was open confused even. It was then that I decided to take the irrational decision to escape the asylum. I moved toward the gate opening it and began to run out. I ran across the muddy wet field, my feet soaked from the wet grass. I could feel the sweat was pouring from my face, my heart pounding. It felt wonderful feeling the cold fresh air the breeze across my face. I stopped to gaze at the beautiful mountains ahead of me. I could see my town clearly from the distance; I could see the tunnel bridge I would walk under to go to school the thatched cottage houses of my friends and neighbours. As I ran with all my might with the asylum well out of my view. I had to plan my next steps to go home and face the wrath of my father, who would very unlikely let me stay despite all my pleas. The other option which I always envisioned when leaving was staying with my cousin Yvette who owned a laundry business in town, and at least then she could let me stay with her and work in the laundry for a while. Whilst I contemplated my next steps it began to rain heavily. Thundery showers drenched my clothes and I was shaking, cold, frightened, and unsure of what was to happen. This will never work I thought. As I reached the tunnel In my home village I saw a black cab flash as it stopped whilst passing through the tunnel. The driver pulled down the window. Instantly I thought it might me one of the guards or even worse Sister Teresa or Sister Mary coming to take me back. I began to run away when all of a sudden a voice shouted "Wait Martha come back." I turned round in awe I instantly recognised the voice of my old primary school teacher Mrs Martin. As I walked towards the cab and she ushered me in, she looked the same as she always did. She had fair complexion big bright blue eyes with curly brown hair. Mrs Martin was always a warm and caring teacher who made every child feel like an individual and important. "Martha I know where you have been all these years and I don't care what happened but right now I am taking you to my home." I was delighted to see Mrs Martin I felt like a child again I felt protected. Mrs Martin drove me to her small cottage home where she resided with her sixteen year old daughter Emily. I was weary at first knowing that my house was only two blocks away from Mrs Martins house, but unsure of her plan. Mrs Martin brought me into her beautiful spacious cottage, where I was given a fresh change of clothes and a warm cup of tea. I explained to Mrs Martin how I felt imprisoned in the asylum, and all of the torture I had been subjected to with the nuns, also I discussed my plans to stay with my cousin Yvette. "You can stay with me the next week. She began. I know your family may not accept you back. I feel you need to rest here get some sleep, and then we can both decide on your next plans. Right now no one will know you're here." She beamed smiling at me. "Why are you helping me I don't want you to get into trouble this is my mess!" I pleaded. "I want to help you don't deserve to be treated with cruelty anymore, if you go back you'll never come out, you have to stay here I must protect you" she pleaded. It was later on that I discovered that Mrs Martin was a strong feminist and had taken part in many protests regarding equal rights of women in Ireland, in relation to employment and education.

The next five days I resided in Mrs Martins house. I slept in a comfy double bed in her spare room with clean fresh sheets and blankets, and carpeted floors, not cold rotten creaking floorboards. Mrs Martin had cooked me warm meals, warm porridge for breakfast, roast dinners, ice cream. It felt wonderful to be supported and to have the nourishment I had been deprived of in the asylum. When Mrs Martin was working she left me alone in the cottage with a range of literature Charles dickens, war literature, biographies a range of books to keep me occupied and escape my current troubles. Mrs Martin had advised me that she thought I could possibly stay with her longer and she had a friend in Birmingham England, who could enrol me onto a hairdressing course at her salon, so I could earn money and she would be able to accommodate me. Travelling to England and being alone in a country did frighten me but then Mrs Martin advised she would visit my cousin Yvette and question if she could help me.

On the fifth day of staying with Mrs Martin her daughter Emily returned from her school trip to knock. I waited in the dining room worrying about Mrs Martins daughters reaction to a fallen girl staying in her house. Emily swung the dining room door open shouting at Mrs Martin, "How can you let her stay her Ma she's a tramp, they're all crazy in that place she's dangerous" She screamed. I stood up, "I think I should get my things and leave here" I said anxiously. Mrs Martins face filled with anger turning red. "Martha is staying here, she has been treated like a prisoner in the asylum she is a good girl and needs my help , she is staying here for as long as I can help her and you won't stop me!" Emily pushed Past Mrs Martin running upstairs slamming the door. "She won't stay here I'll report her" She wailed. I felt myself shaking with fear as Mrs Martin walked towards me holding onto my shaking hands, assuring me she would talk to Emily and make sure she would keep my presence here a secret.

Unfortunately my greatest fears were conformed the next day as Emily had told her school principle I was at her mother's house. The school principle had decided to ring the nuns at the asylum who sent the guards to get me. I was startled and terrified as I heard the guards bang the front door, "we are looking for Martha Egan we have reports she is here open up now" shouted the angry voice. Mrs Martin appeared in the dining room from cooking in the kitchen. "Hide Martha run upstairs hide under the bed in my room lock the door" She enforced shaking. I quickly ran downstairs and followed Mrs Martins instructions I could hear the guards underneath the floorboards. As they forced their way in I could hear Mrs Martin pleading with the guards telling them I was not in the house lying that I had stayed one day at her house and ran off the next day. She tried to barricade the entrance to the stairs. even grabbing hold of one of the guards arms to plead with them not to go upstairs. The guards had broken down the locked door of the room I was hiding in, ordered me to come out from under the bed and dragged me into their large rolls Royce. I was in the car when I saw Mrs Martin's face she was distraught tears were streaming down her face. She ran after the car and shouted, "I won't give up I will get you out somehow" she shouted. I watched her collapse into a heap on the floor outside of her house as we began to exit the street. Mrs Martin felt defeated I had felt defeated to. I was wearing a warm red jumper and comfortable black trousers and shoes, soon to be send to the asylum to wear my rags and back to my life of being a slave. I felt angry and more determined than ever to fight my way out of the asylum. I did not even care about h the punishment I was likely to endure from Sister Teresa and Sister Mary. How could my life get any worse?

CHAPTER 16: Christmas Day

Christmas day was much more difficult to get through that year following escaping and living with Mrs Martin. I had so many plans that week in place for my future going to live with my cousin Yvette and gaining employment at her laundry and studying for a course so I could finally start my life. I lay in my bed frozen as always we all had an orange placed on our bed on Christmas morning it was traditional seen as 'good will' gesture by the nuns. However most of the girls found Christmas day to be quite emotional bringing back memories of their loved ones and remembering a time of freedom. I missed my family routine at Christmas. Me my parents and brother and sister would all sit in our spacious dining room with my aunts and uncles singing various Christmas songs and after we would watch the wizard of Oz, before sitting down to a beautiful turkey roast prepared by my mother . Christmas day was always my most favourite day except in the asylum it felt like a distant memory. The only positive aspect to come out of spending Christmas day in the laundry was that a day's work in the laundry was cancelled. All of the girls sat in the dining room having basic rations cold soup, cold mash potatoes with sausage and bacon, and on Christmas day we would all receive one biscuit each. This Christmas was no different than others. We sat at the dining table with our meal whilst the nuns sat together on their top table eating their beautiful roast dinner, a hot meal we all had longed for. I could s smell the luxurious smell of the gravy as the steam filled my nostrils. The nuns were all dressed in Father Christmas hats and their tables were decorated with an assortment of Christmas crackers and Christmas decoration. It was cruel and spiteful for the nuns to eat their meal in front of us, as some way of making us jealous. This Christmas was different however as in the afternoon I received a visitor by the iron steel gates. As it was Christmas the nuns allowed us to walk the gardens with the guard's supervising us. To my surprise I spotted Mrs Martin standing by the iron steel gates soon she moved around to stand by the tree and I walked over to greet her. "Martha merry Christmas! I have this letter to give you it explains everything, I just didn't want you to feel alone on Christmas day," She beamed. Then a guard charged behind me as I peered through the bush, "What are you doing keep away from the gates" He moaned I turned to greet Mrs Martin "Thank you Mrs Martin for taking care of me that week!" I beamed. Then Mrs Martin handed me the pocket sized letter and scurried away. I went back to my dormitory that afternoon and began to read the letter Mrs Martin sent to me.

Dear Martha,

I want to thank you for staying with me at my home in July. It was a pleasure to have you with me and to see what a hardworking and industrious young lady you have become. I want to apologise for my daughter's behaviour and to inform you that she has been punished for her actions, she had no right to ruin you one chance at freedom. I was shocked saddened and appalled at how you are treated in the Laundry and I believe the longer you stay there the more risks there will be to your physical and mental health. You are a strong determined young lady and I know you will achieve great things once you exit the laundry. I have tried communicating with your parents to try to persuade them to let you leave the laundry but they expressed they would not discuss the matter with me. I would have got you out of the asylum Martha if I had the power but as I am not your relative I am unable to collect you. The way you are being treated in the asylum is a disgrace and you are not a prisoner you are not a criminal you are a good person please do not ever forgot that Martha. I will see you again one day and I want you to know that one day when you will come out of the asylum you are welcome to stay with me until you get on your feet. I also want you to know Martha I will make sure justice prevails!

With all my best wishes

    Mrs Samantha Martin.

I felt intrigued as to what Mrs Martin meant my justice prevailing I wondered if she would report the abuse I reported to her to the police? I also wondered if Mrs Martin would start a protest to release me and the other girls from the asylum, either way her letter filled me with hope and helped me realise I was not alone. Unfortunately the same evening one of the girls in the dormitory Mary Ellen had discovered my letter, and proceeded to send it to Sister Teresa out of jealousy that I had received a message on Christmas day. Sister Teresa proceeded to come to the dormitory and went on to the rip up the letter Mrs Martin wrote to me. "I never read such dribble in my life you really think you will leave this asylum and create a new life. You will be a sinner wherever you go and your too thick to achieve a good educational or to enter a respectable profession, you can only just manage to clean the floors" she laughed, walking away smug in her ability to bring me to tears, although I fought fiercely to prevent them. I vowed that one day when I leave the asylum I will tell everyone how Sister Teresa treated me and I will strive to become as successful as I can be.

CHAPTER 17: Humiliation

I was 25 years old I had been in the asylum for 9 years now. I began to get bored of sports day, there was only so much I could take of hop scotch running and watching the evil nuns laughing and enjoying themselves. This sports day however was to be worse than others, I was about to get a glimpse of what my life could have been had I had not been sent to the asylum, and made that awful mistake on my sixteenth birthday. It was a normal start to the sports day crowds jeered and clapped as the girls played various sports games. Whilst completing the cross country challenge I had witnessed my two old school friends sitting having a picnic with them was a small child. It was Imelda banks and Harriet Simmons my old school friends from my high school. Imelda and Harriet looked so elegant and smart dressed in smart suits with their hair elegantly piled up into neat buns. In comparison I was there in my oversized white dirty gown, greasy short hair scratched knees and a bent posture from hours of working as a slave. I may have been 25 years old but in my body I was 80 years old. I walked up reluctantly to greet them. Imelda smiled at gazed up at me, "Martha it's wonderful to see you we wanted to come and see you". She said patronisingly. What are you both doing now? I quizzed. "I'm working as a primary school teacher I studied English literature at Belfast University before studying for the teacher training programme." "I own my own hairdressers, boasted Harriet I am in charge of 10 staff members and I always get a number of clients every day! She boasted smugly. It felt distressing to see my old school friends here I was a prisoner in the asylum a sinner I had missed out on all of life's mils stones, completing my exams attending the prom, having my first relationship. I had felt almost like a trapped child. Soon Imelda and Harriet threw various questions at me, "What happened to your son?" asked Harriet, "do your parents come to visit you?" Quizzed Imelda. I had felt as if I was a spectacle for the girls a source of amusement for them. Imelda then proceeded to get her make up out of the bag and decided to give me a 'make over' as she put it. I watched as Harriet and Imelda laughed and sniggered as Imelda applied the make up to my face. "There you look perfect said Imelda!" It was great seeing you, "added Harriet. As I walked away from them I felt low and a sense of loss knowing I would never become successful. As I joined the other girls to participate in the egg and spoon race the other girls in the asylum began to laugh at me, even sister Mary and Sister Teresa began to laugh at me as they jeered, 'look at the clown' I ran over to the bathroom only to discover that Harriet had used her make up to give me the appearance of a clown, too bright rosy cheeks, big huge oversized red lips, and a white appearance across my face. I was mortified I ran up to my dormitory room and began to cry myself to sleep.

CHAPTER 18: Sister Teresa

Sister Teresa had always been an abdominal force in the Magdalene asylum, having stayed in the laundry for over 30 years not only had she struck fear into the girls in the laundry she had also created fear amongst the other nuns in the asylum. For years Sister Teresa had bullied me, abused me and taken away my freedom, revelling in shaving my hair humiliating me and making sure I suffered. On Christmas Eve nine years after I first entered the asylum, it was to be the last time Sister Teresa would be seen again. On the morning of Christmas Eve at 7am I heard a shrill scream outside of our dormitory followed by a loud thud. The girls in my dormitory and the others quickly stumbled to their feet to see what had happened. As we reached the foot of the spiral staircase at the bottom was Sister Teresa at the bottom of the stairs laying in a pool of bed. The nuns were sobbing crying as her lifeless body was being cradled by Sister Mary. "Go back to your room girls and don't come out till we say you!" cried Sister Mary. I think at the time all of the girls were in awe and shock over recent events. We all resided in our rooms for longer than usual it was 10am and we still had no breakfast and no laundry service was commenced. After 10 Sister Mary stormed into our dormitory. "Right girls today there is going to be a change of order. I want to inform you all that Sister Teresa has died and Sister Mary has reported that she seen a girl push her down the stairs but was unable to identify who it was. So at 12 o clock all of you will line up outside our office and await an interview with policeman Scot. This is a murder investigation girls and we will find who committed this". Then Sister Mary proceeded to exit the dormitory. I was in shock that morning of course Sister Teresa was an evil women who inflicted suffering on all of us but surely murdering her would be a step to far. As much as I had felt a sense of relief that she had gone, I could not understand why any of the girls would want to land themselves into a heap of trouble and surely suffer a fatal punishment. A half an hour before we were called to interview Lucy Taylor in my dormitory grabbed me by the hand ushering me to the bathroom telling me she must tell me something. As I sat there in the bathroom Lucy began to cry, "I did it" she stuttered. "What did you do" I questioned. "I pushed Sister Teresa down the stairs this morning at 6am. I saw her standing at the top of the stairs and I felt a surge of rage and I ran up and pushed her, and ran back in here before Sister Mary could catch me" she sobbed. "Be quiet you can't let anyone here you, what the hell were you thinking" I warned. "I wasn't thinking Martha I just wanted to hurt her she beat me so hard the other day I was just boiling with anger" she persisted. I held an hysterical Lucy in my arms whilst warning her to not tell anyone or reveal what happened and to say she was not aware of what happened.

As we all lined up at 12 PM I gazed as a nervous Lucy stood in front of me shaking uncontrollably. She stood out a mile at the best of times with long wavy curly red hair,and being six foot she was one of the tallest girls. "You're going to have to carm down or they'll know it's you, just take some deep breaths" I insisted. As I went in to be questioned I was met by the constable Scott a large short policeman, very stern looking and strict. "Where were you in between 6am and 7am?" he quizzed. "In my dormitory sleeping". "What did you hear did you see any one run back to their dormitory ." he stammered. "I saw no one I was in a deep sleep" I persisted. As I left the office I could not believe how quick the interrogation was. I felt sick with fear as I watched a trembling Lucy enter the office I waited nervously outside hoping she would remain carm. One hour had past and I started to feel deep worry that Lucy had admitted what she had done, that she had been foolishly broken. Soon five more policemen entered the office and out came an hysterical Lucy. The officer placed the handcuffs on Lucy and said "I am arresting you for the murder of Sister Brenda Rose" he stated. The officers nearly dragged an unsteady Lucy down the hall she was completely broken. All the other girls in the dormitory gasped in shock as Lucy was led away to face her fate. I had never predicted Lucy would be even capable of murder she had been so shy and meek throughout my time in the asylum. I had observed her fight defiantly with Teresa not to cut her famous long red locks, and Sister Teresa would always brand her 'the freak' dew to her tall appearance in comparison to the other girls. Another girl in the dormitory folded her arms next to me, "at least she got out, she'll probably get treated better there in prison at least shell be warm" She sniggered.

I went to bed that night feeling very anxious and very worried for Lucy now there would be no chance for her to have a normal life and after one foolish action her whole life was to be destroyed. I was also left with the revelation that things were about to change for me in the asylum following Brenda death. Brenda was the leader of the bullying pack of nuns, now that she was gone there would be no hair cutting no more individual taunts. It seemed ironic that the the next day was to be my last day in the asylum, an untimely death was about to be the start of a new beginning for me.

Chapter 19: Freedom

I was 26 now it had been 10 years and 1 month since I entered the asylum. I felt during this time I was still the lost person who entered the asylum completely isolated from friends and family and being treated with such abuse I felt invisible as if I didn't exist. I became immune to being punished in the asylum and ill-treated; it almost became to me a normal part of my existence. I struggled to remember a life without being in the asylum. My brother had arrived in the asylum to release me carrying with him a satchel with clothes for me to change into fresh clothes and a letter to dismiss me to Sister Mary. I remember he stood there in his business suit I awoke to see him standing over me as I lay in the bed. "Martha I've come to get you out, I told you I'd come and get you out one day, and today is the day" I rolled over in the bed to avoid his gaze, "you promised five years ago you were coming to set me free from here and I've been here 10 years what took you so long?" I moaned angrily.

"You have to come home. Da and little Sis passed away last year Martha, Ma is on her own I'm trying to help her but she's falling apart" He cried. I gasped in shock having been unaware of my fathers and sisters passing, "you never came to tell me that they passed away and now you're here asking me to help Ma because you can't cope I won't come" I cried. I was angry and frustrated at my older brother's laizze faire approach, communicating with me as if I had spent my time in a holiday resort. "They died in a car accident Martha I didn't want to tell you as I knew how unhappy you are here please we come back need you!" He pleaded. I put on my new garments my brother gave me a long winters coat and a thatched hat. I grabbed the satchel he gave me I escaped the dormitory as quick as I could, it was 6am and all the girls were sleeping. In the corridor was a new girl Emily who had been sent to the asylum the previous night I could see her cowering in the bed exhausted lost and afraid. I comforted her and hugged her before I left being all too aware how frightened she would be feeling. In the corridor I met Sister Mary. I lowered my head as she continued to fill me with doubt and self dis belief on my exit. "You can't hide behind a hat and respectable clothes, she slithered. Everyone knows you're a fallen woman" She scowled. I refused to turn around to acknowledge her existence and I made my way with my brother behind to exit the front doors. My brother walked us to his black Mercedes car. I knew I was not ready to go home yet I needed time to clear my head time on my own. "Get in the car Martha don't start playing games" he shouted. I turned round as I walked past my brother in his car, "Right now I can't bear to look at you or Ma I just need to be by myself." Despite my brothers constant shouting for me I began to walk towards the field walk towards freedom. It was now 7am it was so quiet walking along the long country road, no cars, no people I could only hear the whistling of the wind, and the rustling of the autumn leaves as I walked peacefully down. I had decided I was still filled with much hostility to my Ma and brother for abandoning me I was not ready to see them to go back to living with them. I envisioned a brand new life living with my cousin Yvette, working in the laundry and following Mrs Martins advice, enrolling on a course and making the most of my life. I had been restricted in the asylum for such a long time I now wanted to finally stand on my own and make my own decisions. As I walked for an hour to my home town I felt very vulnerable. Walking past the houses and shops in my home town I felt that the passers-by knew who I was even with my face covered by the large sun hat I felt bad, I still felt like the fallen girl. To my shock as I came out of the grocery store I met Sara she was smiling looking ecstatic to see me whilst I desperately attempted to avoid her gaze. She walked up to me hugged me forcefully; "Martha it's great to see you, I am so pleased you are out please come over to see us" She contested. I was unable to speak and I reluctantly went home with Sara that afternoon. I was ecstatic Jason was at school I could not face him. "Jason is 10 now he's doing very well at Lady Mount Elementary school we are hoping to put him in for the eleven plus. He is so bright Martha and so athletic he loves playing rugby you must see him" she beamed.

"I have no feelings or desires to meet Jason, I began. I have put that part of my life behind me you adopted him he is your responsibility; you won't be seeing me again." Sara sat on the sofa shocked at my outburst speechless for once that anyone would ever stand up to her. I put on my winters coat only to be met by Sara's husband David in the entry who was now a policeman, "What are you doing in our house he blurted. You're not welcome here, your dangerous, and your to keep away from my wife and family do you understand" he shouted his face contorted in anger. "I am leaving now sir and please do not worry you will never here from me again." I left the house slamming the door. I had no regrets not meeting Jason I would have no role in his life now anyway he was the reason I was sent away.

Irrationally I decided to return to my own house even just to see my mother and say goodbye for starting my new life was something I felt I wanted to do. My brother had left me with a key for our family home I reached my door. I quietly stumbled in. my house was the same as I left it immaculately clean and spotless. I could smell the roast dinner my mother had cooked the night brother. I had noticed all of the family photos on the wall my parents standing proud with my brother on his graduation from medical school, my sister entering her school prom and photos of my family at weddings and parties. All the photos of me were absent it was as if I didn't exist. I went upstairs my room was untouched exactly the same as I remember it. My blue bright coloured wards my soft toy Disney collection placed neatly on my bed, my red sofa chair was still there were I would gaze out the window and write stories. Even my Elvis poster was still up on the wall. I knew however this was no longer a place a comfort, it was a reminder of my childhood which was taken away from me. I walked slowly in the corridor towards my Ma's bedroom. The door was left open slightly I peered through the game in awe at my mother lying in the bed. Ma now had long grey whispery hair her face was wrinkled and grey. She looked peaceful lying in the bed I did not want to disturb her. I went downstairs to the kitchen and proceeded to write my mother note, 'Ma I'm sorry for letting you down I'm sorry for causing you pain. I will come back and see you one day for now I want to be on my own.' I proceeded to quietly leave my house and began to head for the door. That was the last time I was to see my childhood home and my mother again.

I was now tearful upon leaving my family home already doubting my decision to leave my mother a brief note. I went to see my cousin Yvette. To my surprise Yvette now had 3 children and was married to a husband who was in the army. We were both the same age. Yvette had looked so mature now wearing a smart black suit her hair in a neat bob. Yvette had explained that she now left the dry-cleaning business and set up her hairdressing business. To my shock Yvette had ignored and refused my request to stay with her and gain employment to get myself back on my feet. Yvette explained she had a good reputation at the hairdressing company and that my past would attract the wrong sort of attention. Instead Yvette had proceeded to call my brother who drove to the house to 'collect' me. "Come home where else are you going to go" he shouted from the car. I stood and said goodbye to Yvette before she handed me 200 pounds. "listen take this money and get the ferry to England I have a friend their Simone who can offer you free accommodation, and get you involved in voluntary work to get you back on your feet, I will tell her to meet you there" she said reassuringly. I left Yvette's house that afternoon in anger and disbelief that she would not help me I also left my angry and frustrated brother in his car desperate for me to come home. That was also the last time I would see my brother, I just wish now I could have said goodbye properly. I decided I would take the ferry after all, there was nothing left for me in Cork but a broken family unit, a hostile environment and reminders of Jason my son and my punishment. I had felt an overwhelming feeling of loneliness that afternoon so much had changed on my day of freedom, it was not how I imagined it to be. For years I had long to come home be greeted by my parents go back living a normal existence. However with my father and sister passing away, my mother living alone, and my brother working as a doctor. Life was not as it seemed. I was very unsure of my future but certain I could not forgive my mother for abandoning me.

It was now 5pm it was cold and dark and it began to snow. It felt wonderful feeling the snowflakes bristle against my face I had not experienced the snow in ten years. I sat in the café by the ferry eating a warm delicious cheese sandwich, I was salivating at the taste of the warm toasty and savoured every last drop. I felt comforted I had been so used to eating cold food in the asylum it was a privilege now to have warm food a luxury, I enjoyed my freedom that night I enjoyed gazing at the moonlit sky I felt invincible. In the book shop I bought my favourite childhood story Gulliver's travels. I was happy and content. As I sat in the coffee table an hour before the ferry would depart I awkwardly bumped into my mother's friends from our old local parish. Mrs Frigate and Mrs Sargent their hair was blue rinsed they both dressed elegantly in matching floral attire. "I can't believe it, it's you Martha it's really you," Sneered Mrs Frigate. "Well it certainly is good to see you Martha you've been gone for so long you almost became the missing asylum girl," said Mrs Sargent. A large shadow covered me in the table as a lady picked up my suitcase, it was Mrs Martin. "Her name is Martha and she's not lost anymore she's coming home with me!" beamed Mrs Martin.

THE END

Printed in Great Britain
by Amazon